THE VILLAGE THAT VANISHED

Ann Grifalconi   *Illustrated by* Kadir Nelson

Ragged Bears

Author's note

This tale, told in the style of an African folk teller, reflects the way knowledge is passed on traditionally in Africa: through the telling of stories or fables by a local elder or a professional folk teller (often called a *griot*). At night the children gather around an outdoor fire to listen to the storyteller, who, through a variety of ways (riddles, sayings, and tales) weaves a spell over his young audience, always telling the stories in a slightly different way. Thus, it is through the magic and mystery of storytelling that each child discovers the mythology and the history of his or her tribe, and by these parables, learns how to behave in life.

— · —· · —· · —· · —· · —

To the ingenious ways of the past—may they point the way to a future for all!
A.G.

For grandmoms, Verlee and Dorothy, I love you
K.N.

— · —· · —· · —· · —· · —

First published in the United Kingdom by Ragged Bears Limited,
Ragged Appleshaw, Andover, Hampshire SP11 9HX

ISBN 1 85714 251 9

Originally published in 2002 by Dial Books for Young Readers
A division of Penguin Putnam Inc.
345 Hudson Street • New York, New York 10014
Text copyright © 2002 by Ann Grifalconi
Pictures copyright © 2002 by Kadir Nelson

All rights reserved

Printed in Hong Kong on acid-free paper

A CIP record of this book is available from the British Library

For each full-color painting, a pencil drawing was created, which was then photocopied.
Oil paints were then applied to the photocopy.

All the Yao names are authentic, and their pronunciations are noted here.
Abikanile = *ah-bee-ka-NEE-lah;* Njemile = *n-jeh-MEE-leh;*
and Chimwala = *cheem-WAH-lah*

— · —· · —· · —· · —· · —

. . . Gather round, my people, gather round!
And hear the voices of your ancestors
in this tale of courage and of sacrifice.

Young Abikanile waited, still as a bird, in the tall reeds that grew near the water's edge. A butterfly fluttered close by, but Abikanile (whose Yao name means "listen") did not stir. She was listening to her mother's prayers:

"Oh, my ancestor spirits!
Oh, my grandmothers,
Oh, my father, sister spirits!
Hear me now in our need!

"I hear your ancestor voices
Singing in the grass, the trees,
In the winds, the waters . . .
I need your magic!

"Do not deny me now!
Lend me and my children
The secrecy of the crocodile
Below your waters!

"Oh, my ancestor spirits,
We need your magic now!
Protect our village.
Keep us free!"

Abikanile watched her mother rise to her feet. Her tall, strong body was
silhouetted against the red ball of the setting sun. As it sank swiftly behind the line of
trees, she threw a flower offering into the twisting stream that flowed into the dark
forest beyond. . . .

Then her mother (whose name, Njemile, means "upstanding") turned wearily home. Abikanile followed several yards behind, carefully placing her feet in her mother's footprints. *She* knew why Njemile was praying so hard: They might have to leave their homeland—and *soon*.

The slavers were coming!

"These are violent men from the north!" her mother had told her. "They come riding in swiftly on horseback, shooting their long guns, capturing unarmed farmers as they go!"

And Abikanile had heard that sometimes they took Yao children, too.

"But why do they pick on *us*?" she had asked.

"We are a strong people, and hardworking!" Njemile had answered passionately. "They want to sell our labour! Our people are put in chains and sold into slavery to foreign masters!"

It was known that if slavers came, they would begin by capturing those out hunting alone or on guard far beyond the villages. Then they could enter the village itself—and there would be no one who could oppose them!

"So far," Njemile had added, holding Abikanile close, "our own village has escaped—because it is surrounded by forest. But slavers will find it soon enough!"

"What can we do now?" Abikanile asked.

"*Ahh!* I have a plan. . . . If only the rest of our village will listen!"

Now Abikanile wished *she* knew how to pray like her mother, to help give her strength and ideas that could save their village!

When Abikanile and Njemile returned, the villagers had gathered together inside the circle of seven huts that made up Yao. A lookout had just brought the news that slavers had captured people from the nearby villages! No one but he was left, he said, to warn Yao, for Yao's young hunters and distant guards must have been captured as well!

"Ayo!" One elder trembled. "Our strong young men gone and no one to defend us?"

"What are we to do?" the villagers cried. Looking about, Abikanile saw that they were all just women and children, boys and old men.

It was then that Njemile spoke up. "I have a plan. May I speak?"

"Aye!" the elders said, waving her on. She stepped forward, tall and straight.

"We must retreat—disappear like smoke!" she said with quiet force.

"What are you saying, Njemile? We are not magicians, to disappear in a puff of smoke! Do not joke at such a time!"

"I mean we must go into the woods," Njemile explained, "destroying *all traces* of our village, so that the slavers will not know we ever lived here.

"Then they will not follow us, not across the river, not even into the deep forest! And," she ended firmly, *"we must live there until they pass."*

Then Abikanile's grandmother Chimwala (whose name means "stone," and who had remained as silent as one) spoke up. "Yes. To protect our children, you must go swiftly, and soon!"

And so it came about that all the families agreed to Njemile's plan, and prepared to leave. They would take only what they could wear and carry.

But when the villagers came around to help Chimwala, the oldest of the elders, she raised her voice once more.

"I am too slow and old to leave my home! I will remain with my house and our ancestors. The slavers will not take me! Am I not too old and mean? Is it not said: *'The Crocodile will not eat old wrinkled adder snake'*?"

No amount of arguments would move old Chimwala, for her nature was truly stone. Many tried to convince her, but to all these warnings, she cackled: "I will tell them I am a *witch*! They will be so afraid of my magic powers that they will leave this old woman alone!"

Yes, the villagers decided. It would happen like that. To the slavers it would seem old Chimwala was just a hermit, living in a little hut deep in the forest.

So the villagers were agreed. Then one puzzled person called out, "In order to follow Njemile's plan, we must *burn* our village! But such a fire would burn Chimwala's hut down, too!"

"What will we do now?" a scared child asked.

Hearing this, Njemile knew she had not spoken clearly before. "We must disappear *like* smoke, but *not* like real smoke from fires! *That* would attract the slavers' attention from afar!"

"But how, then?" the most anxious elder asked.

"I have thought of the way!" Njemile answered, smiling.

" . . . Each family will have to take apart its own hut, quickly—*stick by stick,
stone by stone*—and bury it, or scatter it in the woods !"

Many villagers gasped. Then one sensible woman suggested, "We can still save
some house poles to use as walking sticks!"

Then another said, "Or to use as tent sticks for our stay in the woods!"

"*Till only the hut of old Chimwala remains!*" said the oldest man, clapping his
hands for them to get to work.

All the women and the strong young girls quickly packed up their great cooking pots, too heavy for the long trek into the woods, and filled them with their most precious things. Then they buried them. One day they would dig them up again!

And the old men and the young boys took the huts apart, *"stick by stick, stone by stone,"* until it was empty space where they had once stood. Then everyone began to clear and rake the area, making it look as if the ground were tilled only for Chimwala's corn.

Soon it seemed Chimwala's hut had always stood alone like that, surrounded only by her vegetable garden and some corn rows.

The people stood back then, leaning on their hoes, their tears wetting the soil where their homes had rested, as the smell of freshly turned earth rose about them.

But now it was Abikanile and Njemile's time to weep and say good-bye. Remaining firm, Chimwala embraced them each in turn, saying only, "I will stay here with the ancestors and we will greet you together when you return."

"May that day be soon!" whispered Abikanile and her mother, Njemile, bowing before Chimwala. They left her and joined the waiting villagers.

Then the people of Yao walked away toward the forest, full of sorrow to be leaving the place where they all had been born. Looking back, they saw old Chimwala in her doorway, sitting as still and silent as a stone.

Walking single file, the villagers travelled along a path that led to the distant forest.
But the wide, quick-running river blocked their way.

"We must cross this river to get to the deeper forest!" spoke an elder.

"But how?" They chattered all at once: "We farmers do not swim!"

"We have no boats!" "The river here is too deep and the current too swift to cross!"

The tribe stood there, defeated by the river. But then the tallest children ran ahead along its shores, trying to find a narrow, shallow stretch of water, where perhaps they could all cross in safety.

Abikanile, being the swiftest, quickly outran the rest. She flew directly toward
the place where she had waited during her mother's prayer.

When she got there, Abikanile saw that the river was narrower, but she could not tell whether it was *shallow* as well! She must test it. But how? She could not swim!

It was then that Abikanile thought: Are we not still in the same ancient woods where every living thing can be inhabited by a loving ancestor?

She thought of her mother's prayer. How did it go? Could she pray, too? The words came flowing through her as she chanted softly:

> *"Oh, ancestor spirits!*
> *Oh, my mother, oh, my father,*
> *Oh, my brother . . . sister spirits!*
>
> *"Hear me now . . . in our need!*
> *. . . Do not deny me now!*
> *I need your magic! . . ."*

Wasn't there a line about water? Ah, yes! Abikanile recalled it now:

> *". . . The secrecy of the crocodile*
> *Below your waters!*
>
> *"Oh, my ancestor spirits,*
> *We need your magic now!"*

Abikanile stopped and listened carefully, hoping for some answer to her prayer. Then she began to feel a coolness upon her cheeks. She heard a stirring. Leaves trembled in a wind that seemed to be coming from within the forest around her.

The surface of the river, whipped by the wind, was beginning to shape into little
waves. They lapped up against round stones that were appearing just above the water!
Soon a row of stones running all the way to the opposite shore was revealed!

Was a stone path really there—or was it only Abikanile's dream? She was afraid it would sink out of sight.

Trying to be at *least* as brave as her grandmother, Abikanile put one bare foot upon a slippery but solid stone . . . and then put the other foot upon the next . . . and the next . . . more and more bravely, until she was *dancing* across the river.

When Abikanile reached the last stone, she called back, "Come! I have found it! There is a path across the water!"

By this time the rest of the people had caught up, only to see Abikanile standing out upon the water. *"Magic!"* they all exclaimed, even her mother. They were afraid Abikanile would suddenly drop out of sight into the rushing waters and drown!

"See?" Abikanile laughed out loud. "It is the stones beneath the water! They run all the way across!"

Then she danced her way back and forth and back again.

"See?" she repeated from the other shore. "It is safe! Come!"

The people gathered at the edge of the river. But they were too timid to trust themselves to the swirling waters.

Lacking faith, *they saw no stones.*

Seeing this, the ancestral spirits ceased blowing upon the waters. Were *these* their children?

Then Njemile the upstanding spoke up once again, scolding: "Have we no shame at all? Are we too afraid to follow? Does it take the sacrifice of an old woman and the bravery of a small child to teach us how to behave?

"Let us go over now, before our foolish fear loses both our tribe and our future!" Saying so, Abikanile's mother put one foot into the water, then another, determined to find the stones because she believed in her daughter's courage.

And the ancestor spirits blew mightily once more, revealing to Njemile each and
every stone beneath the rippling water!

Shamed by their own cowardice and lack of faith, the people began to follow, one
at a time: the old women lifting their skirts, the old men poking their staffs before
them, the children squealing and slipping from stone to stone, until the entire
population of Yao had crossed over!

Then they all came to Abikanile in wonder. "How did you find the path in the water?"

"Like my mother before me," Abikanile answered, looking at Njemile, "I prayed to the ancestor spirits, and they showed me the way!"

Hearing this, her mother hugged her brave daughter to her breast.

Once Abikanile and her people had left the river, they settled deep in the woods, quickly making simple shelters under the trees. For food, the women and small children scattered about, picking berries from the bushes, and nuts from the trees; the old men and boys hunting—catching small animals, and fish from the streams.

And so it went. They knew they would survive. . . .

But had Chimwala survived as well?

The slavers *did* come to the village of Yao (or where it had once stood), riding in, whooping and hollering, firing shots about to frighten all into submission! Suddenly they stopped in their tracks, mouths dropped open, and they lowered their weapons.

For they saw only the single hut, surrounded by tall rows of old corn and crops of beans and yams, newly planted.

Rushing up to the door where old Chimwala sat calmly shelling pea beans, the chief slaver demanded suspiciously, "How is it you can live alone in these woods?"

Chimwala answered with a fierce glint in her eye. "I am a soothsayer! I search for sacred herbs within these woods. . . . I use these for my magic potions!"

But then the man pointed to the newly planted rows. "If you live alone, what about these? They look freshly planted to me! Surely this is much more than you alone could plant!"

Calm as a stone, Chimwala answered, "My distant kin used to come and plant it for me. . . . But now they come no more. I can tend only these few rows."

Not quite convinced, the chief sent his men off to beat the bushes all about, just to be sure there were no people hiding in the woods.

Hours later the exhausted trackers returned, reporting, "There was no one anywhere to be found! We went all the way to the river. . . . There is no evidence of boats near there and there is *no* way anyone could cross to the other side!"

Angry at the loss of slaves he might otherwise have captured, the chief gathered his men to leave, saying, "We have been wasting our time! There is nothing here for us in these woods—and there never was!"

And they rode off on their horses making a great clattering of hoofs never to be seen in Yao again! And Chimwala, sitting in her doorway, watched them go—with a faint smile etched on her stony face.

And that, my children, is how the Yao tribe was saved
and this story came down to us many generations later—
because an old, old woman and a very young girl did what **had** to be done
when their people were threatened. They knew that once the ancestors have
spoken, one must answer not only with faith,
but with courage as well!